X Marks the Spot

Ellen drew a large *X* in the sand. "What do you think the treasure is?"

"Gold coins?" Lila suggested.

"Diamonds?" Jessica said.

"Pearls and rubies?" Ellen put in.

Eva bit her lip and looked worried. "I heard that if you find a treasure from a shipwreck, you have to give it to a museum," she said.

Everyone was silent for a moment. Then Elizabeth spoke up. "Remember what Mrs. Crabby said? Whatever she finds is going to be hers."

"It doesn't sound like she's going to give the treasure to a museum," Todd said.

Jessica gulped. "That means she's planning to steal it. We have to stop her."

D0048753

Bantam Skylark Books in the
SWEET VALLEY KIDS series

SWEET VALLEY KIDS
SUPER SNOOPER #5

THE CASE OF THE HIDDEN TREASURE

Written by
Molly Mia Stewart

Created by
FRANCINE PASCAL

Illustrated by
Ying-Hwa Hu

A BANTAM SKYLARK BOOK ®
NEW YORK • TORONTO • LONDON • SYDNEY • AUCKLAND

RL 2, 005-008

THE CASE OF THE HIDDEN TREASURE
A Bantam Skylark Book / June 1993

*Sweet Valley High® and Sweet Valley Kids are
trademarks of Francine Pascal.*

Conceived by Francine Pascal.

*Produced by Daniel Weiss Associates, Inc.
33 West 17th Street
New York, NY 10011*

Cover art by Susan Tang

*Skylark Books is a registered trademark of Bantam Books, a
division of Bantam Doubleday Dell Publishing Group, Inc.
Registered in U.S. Patent and Trademark Office and elsewhere.*

*All rights reserved.
Copyright © 1993 by Francine Pascal.
Cover art and interior illustration copyright © 1993 by Daniel Weiss Associates, Inc.
No part of this book may be reproduced or transmitted
in any form or by any means, electronic or mechanical,
including photocopying, recording, or by any information
storage and retrieval system, without permission in writing
from the publisher.
For information address: Bantam Books*

If you purchased this book without a cover you should be aware
that this book is stolen property. It was reported as "unsold and
destroyed" to the publisher and neither the author nor the
publisher has received any payment for this "stripped book."

ISBN: 0-553-48064-2

Published simultaneously in the United States and Canada

*Bantam Books are published by Bantam Books, a division of Bantam
Doubleday Dell Publishing Group, Inc. Its trademark, consisting of the
words "Bantam Books" and the portrayal of a rooster, is Registered in
U.S. Patent and Trademark Office and in other countries. Marca
Registrada. Bantam Books, 1540 Broadway, New York, NY 10036.*

PRINTED IN THE UNITED STATES OF AMERICA

CWO   0 9 8 7 6 5 4 3 2 1

To Jonathan David Rubin

CHAPTER 1

A Silver Dollar

Jessica Wakefield finished burying her legs in the sand. Then she patted them smooth. "Look at me," she said, giggling. "No legs."

"I guess we don't look exactly alike anymore," said Jessica's twin sister, Elizabeth.

"That's right. It'll be easy to tell you two apart now," teased their friend Amy Sutton.

Telling Jessica and Elizabeth apart was difficult for most people. The girls were identical twins, which meant that they looked exactly alike. They had the same blue-green eyes and the same blond hair with bangs. Sometimes the only way to tell the twins apart was by checking the name bracelets that they always wore.

Being identical twins made them look the same, but it didn't make them act the same. Each girl had her own special personality. Elizabeth studied hard in school, and liked to read a lot of books. She also liked to play outdoor sports. Jessica didn't like getting her clothes messy and preferred to play inside with her dollhouse. In school, she often whispered and passed notes to her friends instead of listening to the teacher.

But even though they were different in many ways, Jessica and Elizabeth were best friends. And they did have some things in common besides their looks. For instance, they both loved going to the beach. This Saturday they were having even more fun than usual, because their closest friends from Mrs. Otis's second-grade class at Sweet Valley Elementary were there. Amy, Eva Simpson, Lila Fowler, Ellen Riteman, Todd Wilkins, Winston Egbert, and the twins were all members of a mystery club called the Snoopers. But so far, summer vacation had not been very mysterious.

"Look!" Ellen called out. "I found a moon-snail shell."

"A what?" Jessica asked as she finished smoothing out the sand over her legs. "Can you bring it over here? I can't move."

"Sure." Ellen handed her the shell.

"It's beautiful," Jessica said, looking at it from all sides.

"Yeah," Eva agreed. "I've never seen one before."

"That's because they're very hard to find," Ellen said proudly. "I saw a picture of some in my shell book. Now I have one. I can't believe it."

Winston made a face. "Big deal," he said. "It's not like you found pirate gold."

Jessica giggled as she started digging a hole in the sand beside her. Her fingers touched something hard. "Hey!" she shouted. "I think I found something."

Elizabeth helped her dig until the bright sunshine sparkled on a shiny object. Jessica picked it up and rubbed the sand off. "A silver dollar," Elizabeth said. "You found a silver dollar."

Jessica jumped up, spilling the sand off her legs. "A buried treasure," she yelled. "Awesome."

Todd and Winston began digging like crazy. "Maybe there's more," Todd said.

"Maybe it's a pirate's loot," Amy suggested as she joined in.

Soon they were all scooping up sand as fast as they could, using every pail, shovel, and cup in sight. Lila was the only one not searching.

"I already have a real *gold* coin at home," she bragged. "I don't need to dig in the sand for silver." Lila's family was very rich.

"OK, that just means there's more for us," Elizabeth said, laughing.

Winston pointed to some sailboats out on the Pacific Ocean. "Maybe those guys out there are pirates, and they're coming in to get their treasure."

"Not if we get it first," Jessica said.

They all continued digging for several minutes. But aside from a soda-bottle top, empty mussel shells, and lots of rocks, they didn't find anything. "I give up," Amy said at last with a sigh.

"I'm going to show Mom and Dad what I found," Jessica said. She ran to the beach blanket where Mr. and Mrs. Wakefield were playing chess under an umbrella.

"Look!" she said, holding out her silver dollar. The others crowded around.

Mrs. Wakefield looked surprised. "Buried treasure!"

"That's wonderful, Jessica. People often find money and jewelry and other valuable things in the sand," Mr.

Wakefield said. "But it's not easy to find them if you don't have the right equipment."

"What equipment?" Todd asked. "A pirate's map with directions in code?"

"Not exactly," Mr. Wakefield said. He pointed down the beach at a woman in a straw hat who was walking along the water's edge. She was waving a strange object over the sand. "That's a metal detector," Mr. Wakefield explained.

Just then, the woman bent over and began to dig.

"I think she found something," Jessica shouted. "Come on."

CHAPTER 2

Unfriendly Behavior

Elizabeth led the way as the Snoopers raced down the beach toward the woman in the straw hat. They skidded to a stop in front of her.

"What did you find?" Lila demanded breathlessly. "Can we please see?"

The woman looked up in surprise. She was wearing dark sunglasses, and the Snoopers could see curly red hair under her hat. She frowned. "It's none of your business," she snapped.

"We just wanted to know, because my sister found a silver dollar," Elizabeth explained in her politest voice.

The woman frowned even harder. "I don't care what you found," she replied. "I'm busy."

Elizabeth was startled. She couldn't understand why the woman was being so rude and unfriendly.

Todd cleared his throat nervously. "We were wondering how the metal detector works," he said. "Could you show us?"

"No! And don't touch it," the woman said as Winston and Amy bent over to examine the electronic gadget.

"This isn't a toy. Now go away."

"But—" Jessica began.

The woman didn't wait for Jessica to finish. She marched off, but stopped when her metal detector began to make a rapid clicking sound.

"There's something there," Ellen said excitedly. "We'll help you dig."

The Snoopers were about to get down on their hands and knees, but the woman shouted at them.

"Stop bothering me or I'll report you. Haven't you ever heard of giving people their privacy? Now scram—all of you!"

"We were only trying to help you," Elizabeth said. "We didn't mean any harm."

"I didn't ask for your help," the woman said. "And whatever I find is mine, so just leave me alone."

Elizabeth backed up slowly. "We're sorry," she said. "Come on, everybody. Let's go."

As the Snoopers walked away from the woman in the straw hat, Jessica had a stubborn look in her eyes. "Boy, she sure was rotten," she said.

"Yeah," Todd agreed. "She's the rudest, meanest grown-up I ever met. She must hate kids."

"Or really like privacy," Eva said.

Elizabeth looked back over her shoulder. "Or else she's trying to hide something."

The others turned around slowly to stare at the cranky woman in the hat.

"Maybe you're right," Amy whispered, her eyes wide. "Maybe she's up to—"

"Something sneaky," Jessica finished for her. "I think we should find out what it is."

Elizabeth nodded and smiled. "The Snoopers have a case."

CHAPTER 3

X Marks the Spot

"OK," Jessica said. "What we need is a plan."

The Snoopers sat down in a circle on the sand. "I'll keep a lookout on Mrs. Crabby," Winston volunteered.

"That's a good name for her," Todd said. "We should follow her and see if she finds anything."

"What if she's a criminal?" Ellen said. "She could be dangerous bank robber who hid her loot in the sand."

"Psst!" Winston hissed. "Careful, you guys. She's coming this way."

They all watched Mrs. Crabby sit down on her beach blanket and slide something into a canvas bag. Then she set down the metal detector and took off her straw hat and sunglasses. She walked down to the water and splashed in for a swim.

"We've got to check out her stuff," Jessica said.

"But we have to be careful," Elizabeth reminded them all. She stood up. "I've got it—let's pretend we're playing."

"Playing what?" Todd asked.

Elizabeth tagged him on the shoulder. "Freeze tag. And you're it!"

In an instant, the Snoopers were all up and running, chasing each other around the beach. Jessica ran close to Mrs. Crabby's blanket, and then Todd tagged her. She stood "frozen" in place.

Very cautiously, Jessica glanced down at Mrs. Crabby's belongings. A sheet of paper was just visible, sticking out from under the flap of the canvas bag.

"I'll get you, Jess!" Elizabeth yelled, running toward her.

Just then, Winston ran in front of Elizabeth, and they collided. Winston went tumbling across Mrs. Crabby's blanket and fell in a heap on the canvas bag. He jumped up, and the bag spilled open. A map fluttered onto the sand.

"Look," Jessica gasped. "A treasure map."

Elizabeth looked at it closely. "It's just one of the Sweet Valley beach maps you can get at the hot-dog stand," she said. "It shows the beach and the lifeguard stations and the bathrooms."

"I know," Jessica said. "But there are extra pencil marks on it, and a big red X."

"Maybe she has a real treasure map hidden somewhere," Winston said, "and she just copied parts of it onto this map to hide what she's really up to."

Lila ran by them. "Mrs. Crabby is

getting out of the water," she warned. "We'd better get out of here."

They all ran down the beach to a safe distance. When they sat down, Jessica, Elizabeth, and Winston described what they had seen.

"She must have a real buried treasure map hidden," Todd agreed. "It's probably really old and crumbling into dust. That's why she had to copy the important parts onto a new map."

Ellen drew a large X in the sand. "What do you think the treasure is?"

"Gold coins?" Lila suggested.

"Diamonds?" Jessica said.

"Pearls and rubies?" Ellen put in.

Eva bit her lip and looked worried. "I

heard that if you find a treasure from a shipwreck, you have to give it to a museum," she said.

Everyone was silent for a moment. Then Elizabeth spoke up. "Remember what Mrs. Crabby said? Whatever she finds is going to be hers."

"It doesn't sound like she's going to give the treasure to a museum," Todd said.

Jessica gulped. "That means she's planning to steal it. We have to stop her."

CHAPTER 4

Two Clues

"Come on, kids," Mrs. Wakefield called out. "It's time to leave."

The Snoopers looked at each other anxiously, but there was nothing they could do.

"Let's keep this mystery a secret for now," Todd suggested. "Until we have some proof."

"Good idea," Elizabeth agreed. "We shouldn't even tell our parents."

The other Snoopers all agreed. Then they packed up their towels and sand toys, and headed for the parking lot.

"I'm going to the bathroom," Elizabeth told Jessica. "I'll be right back."

As Elizabeth walked across the hot pavement to the restrooms, she passed a row of pay phones. She glanced up and saw Mrs. Crabby's straw hat. The woman was standing with her back to Elizabeth, talking in a low voice.

"I'm sure I was looking in exactly the right spot," she said. "But I'm not sure the metal detector can pick up the gold."

Elizabeth's eyes widened. She tiptoed closer.

"Yes, I know," Mrs. Crabby went on.

"I've been looking a long time, but I'll never give up. *Nothing* can stop me."

Elizabeth could feel her heart pounding. Mrs. Crabby *was* looking for gold. And she had a partner in crime.

Suddenly Mrs. Crabby turned around. She saw Elizabeth, and her eyes narrowed. In a panic, Elizabeth turned and raced to her parents' car as fast as she could.

After they had dropped off all their friends, the Wakefields drove home. "Mom? Dad?" Elizabeth said as she climbed out of the car. "When were there pirates in Sweet Valley?"

"Pirates?" Mr. Wakefield unlocked

the front door. "There weren't any pirates around here."

"But what about the buried gold?" Jessica asked.

"I think I know what you're talking about," Mrs. Wakefield said. "Follow me." She walked into the den and took a magazine from a shelf. It was called *California Coast*.

"Will this magazine tell us if there's any gold?" Elizabeth asked.

Mrs. Wakefield nodded. "Centuries ago, this part of California was controlled by the Spanish, and they took lots of gold and silver back to Spain on ships. Some of those ships were wrecked, so there is some lost treasure on the coast."

As she spoke, Mrs. Wakefield flipped the magazine open to an article entitled, "Golden Splendor in the Sand."

"This is about a research team from the California Museum of Archaeology, right here in Sweet Valley," she explained. "They're digging at a spot they think has many precious artifacts. Look, here's a picture of the researchers."

Elizabeth and Jessica leaned over to get a good look. Suddenly they both gasped. Mrs. Crabby was in the photograph! She was raising one hand to shield her face, as though she didn't want to be seen.

"What is it?" Mrs. Wakefield asked, looking from one twin to the other.

"It's—" Elizabeth began without thinking.

Jessica nudged Elizabeth with one elbow. "Nothing, Mom. It's just exciting," Jessica explained.

Just then the telephone rang, and Mrs. Wakefield got up to answer it.

"We've got to tell the others," Elizabeth whispered as soon as Mrs. Wakefield was out of the room.

Jessica nodded. "But be careful. Remember what Todd said? We should keep this a secret. Mom and Dad would think we're making it up, or else they'd go ask Mrs. Crabby what she's doing, and then she'd know we're after her. Don't you want us to solve this case by ourselves?"

"Yes," Elizabeth whispered. "It feels kind of funny to keep such an important secret from Mom, though."

"We can have a Snoopers meeting tomorrow in the park," Jessica said. "Then we can plan how to get Mrs. Crabby. But remember, we can't tell Mom or Dad anything yet."

"You're right," Elizabeth said. "Until we've got more proof, we have to keep it quiet. Or else Mrs. Crabby might get away."

CHAPTER 5

Lila's Connection

Jessica and Elizabeth rode their bikes to the park the next morning. They took the *California Coast* magazine to show the others.

"You see?" Jessica said as the other Snoopers examined the photograph. They were gathered around the jungle gym for their meeting.

"It's definitely Mrs. Crabby," Todd agreed.

"The caption says 'Archaeology Team, led by Dr. Archibald Reed, explores a site described in a 1792 letter'," Eva read. She looked up. "1792! That's more than two hundred years ago."

Todd slapped his baseball into his baseball glove. "What if there was a *map* with that letter, only Mrs. Crabby got it and Dr. Reed doesn't know?"

"This place they're digging in isn't on the beach," Elizabeth pointed out.

Amy hung upside down by her knees from one bar. "I have an idea," she said. "What if Mrs. Crabby has the map, but doesn't understand it? She could be hanging around the archaeologists to get some kind of clue."

"Maybe there's a clue in the letter," Jessica said. "And she wants to steal that, too, so she can read her map."

Elizabeth sat on the bottom rung of the jungle gym with a worried frown wrinkling her forehead. "I think we should go to the museum and see if we can talk to Dr. Reed. He might know what to do."

"No problem," Lila said, smiling. "My father is on the board of directors of the museum."

"What's a board of directors?" Ellen asked.

Lila blushed. "Um, they have a lot of meetings," she said, sounding confused. "But I bet he can get us a special tour."

"Can he get us in to talk to Dr. Reed?" Elizabeth asked. "We probably shouldn't tell anyone but him about Mrs. Crabby."

"We need some proof, too," Todd said. "Otherwise no grown-up will believe us."

They all nodded in agreement. Lila hopped onto her bicycle. "I'll get my father to call the museum so we can have a tour. I'll call you all when I know."

She rode away. One by one, the other Snoopers climbed onto their bicycles.

"I sure hope we can catch Mrs. Crabby," Jessica said to her sister. "Then we'll be heroes."

CHAPTER 6

Museum Tour

Lila's father arranged for the Snoopers to go on a private tour of the California Museum of Archaeology the following Tuesday afternoon. Elizabeth couldn't wait. When Tuesday finally arrived, Eva's mother picked up all the Snoopers in the Simpsons' van to take them to the museum.

"Remember, kids," she said as they got out of the van. "No touching, running, or shouting. Right?"

"Right," the Snoopers all answered in a chorus.

A bald, thin man came out to meet them. Jessica recognized him from the photograph in her mother's magazine. "Hello, hello!" he called out cheerfully. "I'm Dr. Reed. Welcome!"

"Thank you," Elizabeth said with a smile. "We're glad to be here."

"Thank you for this special tour, Dr. Reed," Mrs. Simpson said.

"Oh, my pleasure, my pleasure," Dr. Reed said, waving his hands and shooing them toward the front door. "Come right this way. Watch your step."

"Remember," Elizabeth whispered to

the other Snoopers as Dr. Reed and Mrs. Simpson walked through the museum's front door. "Be on the lookout for anything fishy."

They entered the museum lobby, walking quietly. Glass display cases stood here and there, with descriptive paragraphs on the walls beside them. The Snoopers spread out to listen as Dr. Reed cleared his throat and got ready to talk.

"Who can tell me what archaeology is?" he asked.

"It's finding buried treasure," Jessica said.

Dr. Reed laughed. "You *could* call it that. But our idea of treasure might be different from yours."

"You dig up pirate gold and jewels, right?" Lila asked.

Dr. Reed pointed to one of the glass cases. "To us, this is much more important and interesting than pirate gold," he said.

Jessica looked into the case and saw a dirty, broken pottery cup and a rusty knife. "*That's* valuable treasure?" she asked in disbelief.

"Yes," Dr. Reed said. "Finding objects used long ago in daily life gives us valuable information on how people used to live."

"But you do have gold, don't you?" Amy demanded.

Mrs. Simpson chuckled. "I guess they

want to hear about shipwrecks and pirates' treasure."

"Well . . ." Dr. Reed glanced around, then lowered his voice. "I'll let you in on a secret."

The Snoopers gathered in closer around him. Jessica wondered if he was going to reveal the location of a pirate's buried treasure chest. She held her breath.

"The secret is, there's hardly any golden treasure around here at all." Dr. Reed smiled mischievously. "You see, this part of California was settled over four hundred years ago by the Spanish. But gold ore wasn't discovered here until just about one hundred and fifty years ago.

By that time, there were no more swash-buckling pirates hijacking ships."

Jessica let out a sigh of disappointment. Perhaps there wasn't any mystery at all.

"Dr. Reed?" Todd raised his hand. "Don't people sometimes find buried treasure at the beach?"

Dr. Reed nodded. "Some treasure washed ashore from shipwrecks. So there's a little bit of treasure out there, but it's rare to find it."

"What if someone had a map?" Elizabeth spoke up.

"A *treasure* map?" Dr. Reed's eyes sparkled. "I don't know about that. Come on, I'll show you the behind-the-scenes part of the museum, where we do our research."

Dr. Reed and Mrs. Simpson talked together as they walked ahead. Dr. Reed unlocked a door marked "Museum Staff Only," and led the way down a long hallway.

"Listen," Jessica whispered to the other Snoopers. "Dr. Reed thought we were joking about the treasure map and buried gold and stuff."

"That's right," Winston agreed. "He didn't believe us."

Elizabeth nodded. "That means he won't believe what we tell him about Mrs. Crabby," she said slowly. "What should we do?"

"I think we should tell him anyway," Eva said.

Far behind them down the hall, they heard a door open. Jessica turned around to look.

She saw Mrs. Crabby coming through a door, holding a tray covered with ancient coins! When Mrs. Crabby saw Jessica watching her, she scowled angrily and hurried away in the other direction.

"It's her," Jessica gasped, as the woman turned a corner and disappeared. "She has some old coins!"

The other Snoopers spun around.

"Where? Who?" Ellen shouted.

"Mrs. Crabby!" Jessica said.

Todd and Amy raced down the hallway, then skidded around the corner. They stopped, looking both ways.

"I don't see her," Todd yelled.

Dr. Reed and Mrs. Simpson hurried back to the Snoopers. "What's all the yelling about?" Dr. Reed asked. "Is something wrong?"

"There's a woman who's trying to steal treasure from the museum," Elizabeth said quickly. "We have to catch her."

Dr. Reed's eyebrows went up. "Oh, *really*?"

Mrs. Simpson looked embarrassed. "I'm sorry, Dr. Reed. They're always making up stories. They like pretending they're detectives."

"But, Mom—" Eva squeaked.

"Please, kids, let's finish the tour and not make any more trouble," Mrs. Simpson said sternly.

The Snoopers looked at each other. They knew Mrs. Crabby was up to no good. But no one believed them.

CHAPTER 7

Digging for Gold

"We'll go to the spot where Mrs. Crabby was digging, and dig there too," Elizabeth said when the Snoopers met at the beach the next day.

"I've got my best shovel," Ellen reported.

"There're eight of us," Todd said. "If we spread out, we're sure to find the treasure."

Jessica shaded her eyes with one

hand and scanned the beach. "Mrs. Crabby's metal detector started clicking hard over there," she said, pointing to a spot about a yard away. "That's where we should dig."

"Ok, let's each pick a spot and get to work," Amy said, holding her spade over her shoulder. "Ready, march!"

Jessica ran over the sand and picked a spot at the edge of the high-tide line. "I'm going to start digging here."

She drew a large square with the edge of her shovel, then began to dig. She piled the sand that she dug up outside the square. Elizabeth was doing exactly the same thing about ten feet down the beach, and Lila was working in a spot ten feet away on the other side.

"What do you think we'll find?" Jessica asked Elizabeth.

Elizabeth shrugged. "I don't know. But whatever the treasure is, we'll have to give it to the museum."

"I bet we'll get a reward," Lila called over. She was throwing the sand over her shoulder as she worked. "A thousand dollars each sounds about right to me."

Jessica's mouth hung open in astonishment. "A thousand dollars? Do you really think so?" she said.

"Sure," Lila answered with a know-it-all shrug. "Or maybe even more. I'm going to buy a horse and new clothes and a new canopy bed with my part of the money."

"Yippee!" Jessica picked up two handfuls of sand and threw them into the air. The sand sprinkled down onto her shoulders, and she laughed. "I'll buy everything at the mall."

Two teenage girls in bikinis walked by, carrying a large portable stereo between them. "What are you all digging in a line for?" one girl asked with a giggle.

Jessica thought fast. "We're making a river," she fibbed. "We're digging a long ditch, and then we'll let the ocean go into it."

The second teenager tousled Jessica's

hair. "You're a cute girl even if you are kind of weird." Both teenagers laughed again as they continued down the beach.

"They won't laugh when we each get a thousand-dollar reward," Jessica muttered.

Winston jogged over. "Did you find anything yet?" he asked.

"Nope," Jessica said. "But it's too soon to give up."

Amy and Eva came running up. "There's someone with a metal detector coming down the beach," Amy reported breathlessly. "She's far away, but I think it's Mrs. Crabby."

"Quick, everyone," Jessica said. "Let's cover up our holes and wait to see what she does. We can't let her know we're after her."

As fast as they could, each Snooper shoveled the sand back into the pits they had dug. Mrs. Crabby was walking slowly down the beach toward them, waving her metal detector back and forth across the sand and staring down at it intently.

"Come on," Elizabeth urged, waving one hand. "Let's hide behind that sand dune."

As Jessica ran, she glanced over her shoulder. Mrs. Crabby was close, but she hadn't seen them yet. Jessica followed the other Snoopers as they dove behind the sand dune and disappeared.

CHAPTER 8

More Silver

Elizabeth carefully peeked up over the top of the dune. One by one, the others popped their heads up to watch too.

Mrs. Crabby stopped and wiped her forehead with one hand. Then she walked over to a spot near where the Snoopers had been digging, and made an adjustment to her metal detector.

Suddenly the machine began to let out a loud, rapid clicking. Mrs. Crabby put down the metal detector and took a small trowel from her bag. She dug quickly in the sand.

"I was digging almost right there," Jessica exclaimed in dismay.

"Let's get her," Amy said.

"Shh!" Todd warned. "Let's watch and see what she finds first."

Elizabeth nodded. "And see if she looks like she's going to keep it to herself."

While they watched, Mrs. Crabby reached into the hole she had just dug and took out two gleaming silver pieces.

"Those are coins," Lila whispered. "Silver coins."

Mrs. Crabby examined the coins carefully, then put them in her pocket. Elizabeth felt a rush of anger. "Hey!" she yelled, jumping up. "You have to give those to the museum!"

Elizabeth rushed down the sand dune with the others right behind her. The Snoopers surrounded Mrs. Crabby.

"We saw you take those silver coins," Elizabeth repeated angrily. "Ancient treasure is supposed to be given to the museum."

Mrs. Crabby glared at them. "Oh, really?" she asked sharply.

"Yes," Jessica said, stepping forward. "Are you going to give those coins to the museum?"

"Or are you going to steal them like you stole those coins from the museum yesterday?" Amy demanded.

The woman let out a sour laugh. "You kids sure think you're smart, don't you?"

"We know what's right and what's wrong," Todd said.

"Well, why don't you take a look at my *treasure,*" Mrs. Crabby snapped. "You'll see if you're right or not."

She reached into her pocket and pulled out some coins. The Snoopers leaned close for a good look. In Mrs. Crabby's hand were two ordinary nickels. Elizabeth turned pink with embarrassment.

"I wonder if the museum would be interested in these," Mrs. Crabby said. "They're pretty ancient. One is from 1980, and the other is from 1989. I'll personally hand them over to Dr. Reed, who happens to be a friend of mine. Maybe he'd be interested in the silver dollar *you* found a few days ago too."

"But—but—" Jessica stammered.

"Now, I've asked you kids to stop pestering me," Mrs. Crabby went on. "And I'll say it again. Just quit meddling in things you don't understand."

Lila stamped her foot. "But you—"

"Come on," Elizabeth broke in, backing away. "We're sorry we bothered you. We're going now."

The other Snoopers looked at Elizabeth in surprise, but they followed her as she led the way back to the sand dune.

"I still think she's after a real buried treasure," Jessica insisted.

Elizabeth sat down and doodled thoughtfully in the sand with her finger. "I wonder," she began with a frown. "Do you think Dr. Reed *is* a friend of hers?"

"She probably just made friends with him to get help with the map," Ellen said.

Lila dug her heels into the sand. "I'll ask my father. Maybe he'll be able to question Dr. Reed and find out how much Mrs. Crabby knows about the treasure."

"Good," Elizabeth said. "I sure hope we can figure it all out."

CHAPTER 9

Abigail Jefferson

Jessica sat in the den after dinner, swinging her legs over the side of the couch and staring at the telephone.

"Lila said she'd call tonight," Jessica complained. "It's getting late."

Elizabeth was making paper airplanes. She carefully creased one fold and didn't answer.

"How can you sit there and make paper airplanes at a time like this?"

Jessica asked impatiently. "Lila might have some important clues for us."

"I know," Elizabeth said. "But we just have to wait. She'll call."

Jessica pouted. "I wish she'd hurry up."

Just then the telephone rang. Jessica sprang up from the couch and pounced before the second ring. "Hello?" she shouted. "Is that you, Lila?"

Elizabeth stood up and put her ear next to Jessica's so they could both listen. "Did you find out anything, Lila?" Elizabeth asked.

"Yes, I did." Lila sounded very mysterious. "You'll never guess what. Mrs. Crabby actually *works* at the

Museum of Archaeology."

Jessica nearly dropped the phone in shock. "Wow! She must be a spy or something."

"Well, I don't think so," Lila said. "She's worked there for ages. And her specialty is ancient coins."

"So she had a reason for carrying a tray of coins," Elizabeth said. "She probably wasn't stealing them at all."

Jessica frowned. "Maybe not. But maybe she has secret information on some buried coins, and she's trying to sneak away and find them by herself. What else did you find out, Lila?"

"Her name is Abigail Jefferson," Lila said. She giggled. "But I still think of her as Mrs. Crabby. She only works at the museum part time because her husband died in a car accident last year."

"That's sad," Elizabeth said.

"I've got it," Jessica said. "Maybe after her husband died, she went nuts, and it turned her into a criminal."

Elizabeth gave Jessica a doubtful look. "That happens only in the movies. I bet she's just sad and lonely, and misses her husband. That's probably why she acts so cranky and mean all the time."

"Maybe," Lila agreed.

"But don't forget," Jessica reminded them. "Liz heard her talking on the telephone to someone, right? She's not working alone. She has a partner."

Elizabeth frowned. "That's true. She even said she wouldn't let anything stop her."

"I say we keep following her," Lila said. "If she gives up, then we have a chance to search for the treasure ourselves. And if she keeps digging and she finds something—"

"Then we've got her," Jessica said gleefully.

"Let's call the rest of the Snoopers," Lila said. "I'll tell them to meet us at the beach tomorrow."

After they hung up, Jessica and Elizabeth went to find their mother.

"Can you take us to the beach again tomorrow?" Elizabeth asked.

Mrs. Wakefield looked surprised. "Again? You two are turning into real beach bums. Isn't there anything else you'd like to do?"

Elizabeth and Jessica looked at each other. "No, Mom," Jessica said. "There's nothing we want to do more than go to the beach."

CHAPTER 10

Striking Gold

The next morning, Elizabeth was in the kitchen packing some sodas into the cooler to take to the beach. She heard a clanking sound coming from the garage, so she opened the back door to see what it was. She saw Jessica putting some gardening shovels into the trunk of the car.

"I don't think Mom will let us take those," Elizabeth said.

Jessica slammed the trunk shut and brushed off her hands on her shorts. "Sure she will. Come on."

All the way to the beach, Elizabeth sat on her side of the backseat and thought about Mrs. Jefferson. Elizabeth thought it was sad that Mr. Jefferson had been killed in a car accident. It was no wonder Mrs. Jefferson was grouchy. But if she was a crook, they still had to catch her.

"Here we are," Mrs. Wakefield said as she pulled the car into the parking lot at the beach. "We can't stay here all day this time. I have homework to do for my decorating course."

Elizabeth sent Jessica a worried glance. How much longer could they keep tailing Mrs. Jefferson?

"What if nothing happens again?" Elizabeth whispered to her sister. "We can't ask Mom to bring us to the beach every single day."

"Don't worry," Jessica said confidently. "I feel lucky."

When Mrs. Wakefield opened the trunk to take out the beach umbrella, she let out a cry of astonishment. "What are all these tools doing in here?"

Jessica hurried over to grab the shovels. "We're making a big sand castle today," she explained, dragging them out. She nudged Elizabeth.

"Right," Elizabeth said. "Our regular beach shovels aren't good enough."

The other Snoopers were already on the beach, armed with shovels and spades and pails. "Spread out, everybody," Jessica said. "We've got to find that treasure today."

"Maybe we'll all even get on TV if we find it."

Winston said. "We'll be famous."

"Real heroes," Amy said.

"It's pretty exciting, isn't it?" Eva asked Elizabeth as they set to work.

"I guess so," Elizabeth said quietly. She was still thinking about Mrs. Jefferson's husband.

Before long, the Snoopers had dug a ditch ten feet long, two feet wide, and one foot deep. The sand that they were digging out of it was piling up into a mountain. Other people on the beach stared as they strolled past.

Mrs. Wakefield came over to put some sunblock on the twins' shoulders. "What on earth are you up to?" she asked.

"It's the sand castle, Mom," Jessica said. "This is the moat."

"You should start on the castle itself if you want to finish before we have to leave," Mrs. Wakefield said. She headed back to the blanket where she was sitting with Mrs. Sutton and Mrs. Simpson.

A few minutes later, Amy dropped her shovel and fell to her hands and knees in the ditch. "There's something here," she said, scooping up sand with her fingers.

The Snoopers quickly gathered around her. They watched as Amy reached into the sand and pulled with all her might. Finally she yanked a rusty bicycle chain out of the wet sand.

"Some great treasure," Lila said, rolling her eyes. She folded her arms over her chest. "I'm getting tired of this."

"Me, too," Ellen agreed grumpily.

Todd picked up his shovel and jabbed

it into the bottom of the ditch a few times. "Maybe this case was a big mistake," he muttered. Then his eyes widened. "Hey! I see something gold."

CHAPTER 11

Charms of Gold

Jessica leaped into the ditch beside Todd. "What is it?" she asked. "Is it really gold?"

Todd carefully scraped away the sand. "I think so." While the Snoopers looked over his shoulder, Todd picked up a gleaming gold chain with dozens of gold charms on it.

"A charm bracelet," Ellen whispered. "This is great."

Winston made a face. "Big deal. A charm bracelet."

"But it's gold," Jessica said. "We really found a real buried treasure. Here, Todd, let me look at it."

Jessica sat on the edge of the ditch, holding the charm bracelet in both hands. Lila, Ellen, Elizabeth, and Amy sat around her, admiring the charms.

"Look, there's a teapot," Lila said. "And a pair of ballet shoes."

"And a poodle," Eva said. "It's so cute."

"And a miniature telephone," Jessica said.

"Do you think this could really be old and rare?" Amy asked.

Winston laughed. "Get real, Amy. They didn't have telephones in the olden days."

Elizabeth touched a round medal with a rippled edge. "There's writing on this charm," she said.

Jessica turned it over in her palm. The sunlight flashed on the medal as she squinted to read the swirly engraved letters.

"It says 'With all my love, P.J. to A.J., May 12, 1989,'" she read slowly.

"Hey," Elizabeth said. "A.J.: Abigail Jefferson."

"That's just a coincidence," Lila said.

"Right," Jessica agreed. "It doesn't mean anything. Lots of people have those initials. I'm going to try it on."

Just then a shadow fell over them, and a shocked voice said, *"Where did you get that?"*

CHAPTER 12

The Big Reward

Stunned, the Snoopers turned around. Abigail Jefferson was standing behind them. But instead of her usual crabby expression, she was smiling with joy.

"I've been searching for that bracelet for months," she said, reaching out to take it.

Jessica quickly closed her hand around the treasure and backed up.

"Is this what you had the secret map for?" Todd asked Mrs. Jefferson. "We saw the red *X*, so you have to tell the truth."

Mrs. Jefferson looked startled. "Well, I did have this placed marked on a map, yes."

"Aha!" Lila shouted in triumph. "So you *did* have a treasure map."

"You *were* going to turn this over to the museum, weren't you?" Jessica asked.

"Just because you work there doesn't mean you get to take things that belong to them," Amy added. "Like *coins*."

To everyone's surprise, Mrs. Jefferson began to laugh. The Snoopers stared at her in silence.

"You crazy kids," Mrs. Jefferson said. "I don't know what you think I've been doing, but that bracelet belongs to me. My husband gave it to me on our thirtieth anniversary. That's why there are thirty charms on it. I lost it here some time ago, and ever since my husband died, it was even more important for me to get it back." She stepped forward with her hand outstretched.

Slowly, Jessica held out the bracelet. She gave Elizabeth a questioning look, and Elizabeth nodded. Jessica dropped the charm bracelet into Mrs. Jefferson's hand.

"But what about those coins you took from the museum?" Amy asked.

"I study ancient coins," Mrs. Jefferson explained with a smile. "The ones you saw me take were part of some research I'm doing at home."

The Snoopers looked at one another in embarrassment. Their mystery seemed to be dissolving into thin air.

"But wait a second," Elizabeth said. "You had a partner. I heard you talking on the pay phone."

Mrs. Jefferson frowned in disapproval. "I must say, I really don't like being spied on. But just so you know, I was talking to my daughter."

"Your daughter?" Jessica repeated faintly.

"My daughter," Mrs. Jefferson said.

"And by the way, she was getting worried that I was turning into a crabby hermit."

Elizabeth blushed bright red. She was glad that Mrs. Jefferson didn't know what the Snoopers had been calling her behind her back.

"You were pretty grouchy," Ellen whispered. Eva shushed her quickly.

"Well," Mrs. Jefferson said. "I apologize for being so cross with you. I was afraid someone else would find the bracelet and I would never get it back. And I suppose that if you were trying to protect the museum, I should be glad about that. I'm also very glad that you kept hunting and found my bracelet."

"So there wasn't really any Spanish treasure, or pirate's gold, or anything really valuable like that," Jessica said with a sigh.

"Yes there was," Elizabeth corrected her, giving Mrs. Jefferson a smile. "I think we found something priceless."

Jessica grinned. "Yeah, I guess you're right. Maybe we're pretty good detectives after all."

SWEET VALLEY KIDS

Jessica and Elizabeth have had lots of adventures in *Sweet Valley High* and *Sweet Valley Twins*...now read about the twins at age seven! You'll love all the fun that comes with being seven—birthday parties, playing dress-up, class projects, putting on puppet shows and plays, losing a tooth, setting up lemonade stands, caring for animals and much more! It's all part of SWEET VALLEY KIDS. Read them all!

☐ JESSICA AND THE SPELLING-BEE SURPRISE #21	15917-8	$2.75
☐ SWEET VALLEY SLUMBER PARTY #22	15934-8	$2.99
☐ LILA'S HAUNTED HOUSE PARTY # 23	15919-4	$2.99
☐ COUSIN KELLY'S FAMILY SECRET # 24	15920-8	$2.99
☐ LEFT-OUT ELIZABETH # 25	15921-6	$2.99
☐ JESSICA'S SNOBBY CLUB # 26	15922-4	$2.99
☐ THE SWEET VALLEY CLEANUP TEAM # 27	15923-2	$2.99
☐ ELIZABETH MEETS HER HERO #28	15924-0	$2.99
☐ ANDY AND THE ALIEN # 29	15925-9	$2.99
☐ JESSICA'S UNBURIED TREASURE # 30	15926-7	$2.99
☐ ELIZABETH AND JESSICA RUN AWAY # 31	48004-9	$2.99
☐ LEFT BACK! #32	48005-7	$2.99
☐ CAROLINE'S HALLOWEEN SPELL # 33	48006-5	$2.99
☐ THE BEST THANKSGIVING EVER # 34	48007-3	$2.99
☐ ELIZABETH'S BROKEN ARM # 35	48009-X	$2.99
☐ ELIZABETH'S VIDEO FEVER # 36	48010-3	$2.99
☐ THE BIG RACE # 37	48011-1	$2.99

Bantam Books, Dept. SVK2, 2451 S. Wolf Road, Des Plaines, IL 60018

Please send me the items I have checked above. I am enclosing $_____ (please add $2.50 to cover postage and handling). Send check or money order, no cash or C.O.D.s please.

Mr/Ms _____

Address _____

City/State _____ Zip _____

SVK2-4/93

Please allow four to six weeks for delivery.
Prices and availability subject to change without notice.

A BANTAM SKYLARK BOOK

FRANCINE PASCAL'S
SWEET VALLEY Twins AND FRIENDS ®

Buy them at your local bookstore or use this handy page for ordering:

Bantam Books, Dept. SVT3, 2451 S. Wolf Road, Des Plaines, IL 60018

Please send me the items I have checked above. I am enclosing $_____
(please add $2.50 to cover postage and handling). Send check or money
order, no cash or C.O.D.s please.

Mr/Ms _____

Address _____

City/State _____ Zip _____

SVT3-4/93

Please allow four to six weeks for delivery.
Prices and availability subject to change without notice.